ESCAPE FROM ETERNITY
FIONA D. MAHADKAR

Author's Message:

For those seeking a break from monotony, this is the perfect escape. Dive into a world where boredom is a foreign concept, as this book offers a thrilling blend of complexity in plots and settings, unveiling suspense in every chapter. Whether you enjoy a variety of genres, this story caters to diverse tastes, featuring paranormal activities, intense fights, self-resilience, and more. The journey promises excitement and surprises. Upon reaching the end, discover an acknowledgement page and insights into the author.

Enjoy the ride!

Table of contents:

Meet the characters:

- Abby
- Ellie
- Sarah
- Francesco
- Avery
- Sun Goddess
- The Guardian
- King of Hell
- Earth Fairy
- Air Fairy
- Fire Fairy
- Water Goddess
- Heaven Queen
- Riddle Castle
- Avery's Ghostly Friends

1

Abby and Ellie

The rumors about the portal of eternity didn't budge to Abby until now. When it was said to reopen again, she didn't believe it until — it was her to experience.

FRIDAY EVENING, "Abby" Ellie spoke as they sat on the bed, "have you noticed anything strange about the people of Mischief County?" Abby wasn't focusing on what she was saying until she realized she was talking about THE PORTAL.

Snapping out of her deep thoughts and setting aside her book before replying to Ellie. "Yes Ellie, I've seen something odd about them like they are possessed by *something* or *someone*." She again picked up her book and started reading.

Abby noticed peasants who were walking down the street looked awkwardly scared. They started to run suddenly, not wanting to get out of their home, abandoning their pets (which to Abby felt bad for them), and rushing around for everything.

"Abby!" Ellie said sheepishly.

"Uh — yeah?"

"The news is worse than you think it is. Follow me!"

Abby set aside her book, this time closing it with her bookmark, and rushed over to follow her friend. What Abby realized when they got to the designated location, was just a lonely mirror standing by itself.

"Ellie! It is just a mirror! What is the connection between the actions of the people and this mirror?"

Ellie stood there blank and Abby doubted her as if she was constantly having her name repeated in her head. "Ellieee!" she screamed again. This time Ellie turned around and then said "Save me please!" before throwing herself into the mirror.

Seeing her friend leave, Abby muttered those words in her head again and again. As she started to put the puzzle pieces together, she understood that there could be only one meaning to this: The mirror isn't just a mirror, but the portal itself.

2

Rescue Plan

SATURDAY MORNING, Abby woke up with a loud yawn. She put on her pink fluffy slippers and walked to her bathroom to freshen up. Today she was supposed to wear her favorite pink floral dress but instead wore her turquoise hoodie and denim ripped jeans.

She drank some hot coffee, grabbed her book and a pen, and then took off to go to the park. There she sat on one of an empty bench and looked up at the kids playing. The bench next to her was an old lady reading a newspaper and a younger woman sitting next to her chatting with someone.

Abby closed her eyes and took a deep breath before returning to work. It was a lovely early morning breeze as it rubbed against her skin. She didn't want to go inside the portal but she knew she had to save her friend. "Okay," she said to herself, "let's do this."

It was two hours before Abby decided to head home. She looked super stressed out and most probably under the weather. Upon reaching home, Abby threw her stuff on the couch and slammed herself on the bed. The only thing she could think about was 'how to save Ellie, her dearest friend'?

It turns out, five years ago, her most beloved family members sacrificed themselves to save Abby. After that, THE PORTAL became her greatest fear, and losing her best friend made her heartache. She sighed and kept reminding herself to calm down. One thing she didn't know for sure was, if there could there be an exit to escape from eternity. Could she fix the past and save her family? Those questions raced across her mind like a flashing thunderstorm.

Not knowing what to do and bursting into tears, she ordered some pizza from Domino's. Ting dong! And the delivery guy arrived moments later. "Thanks! How much?" The delivery guy didn't reply and left. She was dazzled at his actions and closed the door worriedly. After eating she set out to her cousin Sarah. In her eyes, she could see that Abby was troubled and wasn't sure if she should ask anything of Abby and just motioned her to come in.

"What happened Ab?" Abby looked like she was going to completely tear out before explaining anything to Sarah. Amid her lines, she would start crying or sometimes even feel that she should run away from eternity. But how could that be possible, after all her family did for her? No, she shouldn't. The constant fight between pain and courage made her uncomfortable, and she did not want to say a single word about anything.

After Sarah heard all parts of the story, she didn't know what to say. Instead, she wrapped herself around Abby like how a mother would do when her child was in pain and agony. She invited her for a sleepover and said that they would plan out everything in the morning — together.

Abby could only force herself to smile barely in a comforting way. At least there was one person who was on *her* side.

SUNDAY MORNING, "Rise and shine Abby..." Sarah sang. Abby rubbed open her eyes to see Sarah holding a tray with flowers, coffee, and pancakes. Yum... that is Abby's favorite snack. She sat on the bed next to her and put the tray in the center. "This is all for you, Miss Abby!" Abby beamed. "Thank you!" she managed to say.

After getting fresh the two head to the couch. It was 10:00 am in Mischief County. "Sooo..." Sarah interrupts Abby's thoughts. She shot a glance before looking to the side. "What are we planning to do, Miss

Abby?" Abby showed the plan she made and then spoke back to Sarah, "This is the plan I made yesterday, but of course, we may also need a backup plan." Abby handed the book to Sarah and she took a closer look before saying, "Ah... interesting. Perhaps you are correct, Miss Abby."

Abby knew that Sarah was teasing her as she had known since the beginning that she hated being known as 'Miss Abby'.

3

Abby and Sarah

11:00 AM, MISCHIEF COUNTY, AT SARAH'S PLACE, "Can you *please* stop calling me 'Miss Abby' Sarah?" Sarah started chuckling. "What's so funny?" Abby asked her enthusiastically. "Stop it Ab, you know I'm just joking around!" Sarah said with a mouthful of chips. Abby frowned. She sighed and then shook her head in frustration. "FOCUS!" Abby snapped. "Whoa, cool down Abby. What is the point of—." Abby didn't let her complete her sentence and instead sharply replied, "Ugh, don't you know that this is an important quest, Sarah!?" Sarah blinked her eyes then sighed, waving her hands by her face. "Yeah, I guess you're right Abby."

Abby laid a poster sheet on the nearby table and labeled it 'ABBY'S AND SARAH'S QUEST'. "Fancy!" Sarah said, eyeing the sheet. Abby gave her an approving nod. "Okay, let's begin!" She wrote down something, and Sarah looked nervous and at this point, she started twiddling a strand of hair and biting her thumb.

"So," Abby started to say, "First thing is first. We are going to need a survival kit. What should we include? Let's start brainstorming." After moments of brainstorming, they came up with twenty important stuff they would need on their journey. "Perfect!" she said happily. "Let us continue to plan!" Sarah nodded.

Three hours passed and now it was 1:15 pm in Mischief County. Abby's stomach had already started rumbling. "*Grr*", it said. "Was that you Ab?" Sarah asked her worriedly. "Yeah, I'm hungry, how 'bout you?" Sarah nodded, "Yeah, me too! What should we eat? How about Mexican Rice with Tostadas?" Abby smiled sarcastically.

After the girls had finished eating, it had already been past an hour and fifteen minutes, which meant that it was now 2:30 pm in Mischief County. Abby shuffled her nose while muttering some words under her breath. "Okay," she said, "THE PORTAL is down in the basement at my house, and it normally opens up at 7 p.m. which means we have about four hours to prepare what we need. If we don't hurry now, then we won't have enough time, so let's go in my car."

Both girls followed each other out the door, into the car, and drove back to Abby's place.

4

Into The Portal We Go!

*Narrator: Sarah followed Abby to her room where they started to prepare their necessary needs, but will the mission truly be successful? Will she be able to save the past and escape eternity? Now you see dear readers, when Abby and Sarah step foot into THE PORTAL OF ETERNITY, things don't go as planned. What could happen? The girls had no idea. *

4:20 P.M., AT MISCHIEF COUNTY, ABBY'S PLACE, "Okay we are going to need something light yet portable for both of us." Abby urged Sarah to look within the house while gathering everything they needed. Eventually, when the girls were ready to go in, Abby tapped the mirror with her hand. "Here goes nothing!" she said with a deep breath. The girls stepped in.

The portal swirled with vibrant colors that flashed in a blink of an eye. As Abby and Sarah step foot inside the portal of eternity, a sudden urge of energy pulsed through the air. The surroundings transformed, transporting them into a realm that neither girl had ever seen before.

The girls found themselves in a vast, desolate landscape with distorted reality. Time seemed to lose its grip as past, present, and future intertwined. The very fabric of existence appeared unstable and unpredictable within this otherworldly dimension.

As Abby and Sarah ventured deeper into the realm, they encountered strange beings and encountered bizarre phenomena. Reality shifted continuously, making it hard for them to navigate and trust their senses. They realized their mission to save the past and escape eternity would not be as straightforward as they had anticipated.

The portal's power begins to affect their minds, distorting their thoughts and memories. The girls struggled to distinguish what was reality and what was an illusion. They faced their deepest fears and unresolved traumas, which manifested as formidable challenges blocking their path.

Additionally, the cosmic forces guarding the portal sensed their presence and sought to prevent them from alternating the course of time.

An illusion of a black wall and mirror appeared before them causing them to startle. Both girls faced back-to-back and circled in every possible direction. As they did Abby spoke to Sarah. "Legend has it," she says restlessly, "The Guardian of the portal has a time clock which we can use to fix the past!" Sarah's only reaction was scared and she barely managed to say, "Phew! If we can somehow get our hands on it, we can be out of here in no time!"

Just as she finished speaking, a bright light flashed causing them to close their eyes. When they opened it, they were standing in front of two stone giants. Giants were one of Sarah's deepest fears. She was nearly about to faint when Abby said "It was an illusion to see how we'd surpass the challenge!" She rolled her eyes and said, "Oh right I forgot but you know it."

5

Let's Settle Things Please!

*Narrator: The two go into the mirror and start to feel weird energies and forces. The challenge was to go to the guardian and seek to get the time clock. But to get there was a very difficult task and almost impossible to reach there. According to legend, Abby and Sarah had to surpass different challenges and prove to the guardian that they were capable of completing the task. Will they be able to manage it? *

IN THE REALM OF THE GUARDIAN, when everything was over a large stone gate appeared before their eyes. It opened to a realm different from the others they had seen. To Abby, it seemed like the gate itself wanted to open for them as if it knew that they wanted to enter. Without any hesitation, the two stepped in.

As Abby could have ever imagined, the realm was covered with a golden interior, white puffy clouds covering ceiling décor, golden statues that were in the shape of angels, and emerging bright golden light coming out of the throne room.

There sitting on the throne was a white statue. Unlike any other statue, this statue had a pale white marble stone surface, long hair reaching up to whoever was sitting on it, and clothes that had Greek design. Abby could not believe her eyes! It was an incredible view! Abby wondered why they were sent here in *this* particular realm.

A golden-yellow light shone and out spoke a voice. It was harsh and seemed very mad, at least that's what she thought. "Who DARES to enter this room without my permission!? What do you want!?" Looking at Sarah, she could see that *the voice* was frustrated. "We are Sarah and Abby," Sarah said as if nothing had happened. As Sarah continues to introduce themselves, Abby eyes a celestial ball. It looked like it held the time clock they needed. Her gaze fell upon the majestic man who looked like he hadn't been there when they arrived. He goes to the throne, bows down, and then whispers something in the ear of the supposed Guardian. He nodded his head and left through the golden gates. As he approached closer, Abby could see that it wasn't a regular man, but a satyr.

"So, tell me Abby and Sarah, why do you wish to get the celestial golden clock to reverse time and fix the past?" The girls stood there as if they had just heard a blanket statement. Abby sniffed out tears as she explained what had happened in the past and why their purpose was to come and seek for it. "Hmm..." the Guardian said, scratching his beard. Of course, he had pity on the girls, but he couldn't trust them, could he?

He once again called the satyr into his realm and muttered something to him. The satyr nodded in agreement and then left. After a while or so, he returned to the realm only this time holding an ancient will. The Guardian takes the will and begins reading it to himself. He scratched his beard a little more before handing it back to the satyr. Again, the satyr bowed down and left.

"As per the ancient script of ancestry, I cannot hand over the celestial weapon. However, I will be able to give you the weapon if you are worthy enough. Once you've earned it, you will have three days to go back in time and fix it. One rule you must remember though is the time here won't be the same as the time there. Follow this golden map and it will be your first challenge if you both accept."

The Guardian finished his sentence and gave the map to Abby. Although the Guardian had given them enough information, Abby still had one question in her mind. "O great Guardian, if we ever need any help, who to call? And what do we call them?"

There was a long moment of deep silence before the Guardian spoke again, "Well my child, that indeed is a good question. You are going to have to call the Great Satyr from the Satyr tribe. One will come to assist you, but remember, that you can only request him three times. After that, if you fail to follow these rules then you'd fail the mission. So! Choose wisely. You may be dismissed!"

*Narrator: The girls take the map given by the Guardian and thank him for his help. The fun part of the story will begin with their first challenge. Along with the map they carried, the Guardian also gave them a conch to call for assistance when needed. *

6

Sarah Got This

Challenge #1, The golden gate opened once more for the duo. Abby confidently took the lead as Sarah followed leisurely. Upon reaching the gate, they encountered a fork in the path. The upcoming challenges required to navigate correctly, choose the right door and illuminate the Sun Goddess's heart.

Obstacle 1, "Abby, does the map provide any guidance on which path to select?" Abby examined the map from various angles but found no clues. "Unfortunately, it doesn't... However, we could utilize the conch to seek assistance." Abby suggested. Sarah vehemently shook her head and replied, "No! We mustn't do that!" Surprised, Abby asked, "But why?" Sarah explained with conviction, "Because if we use one now, we will have only two remaining! What if the upcoming challenges prove to be more challenging than we anticipated? We might genuinely require all of those opportunities!"

Abby could perceive the unwavering resolve resonating in her voice as she spoke, "Very well, I acquiesce. It appears that your judgment is sound," Sarah bestowed upon her nod of affirmation. Unbeknownst to Abby, Sarah discreetly retrieved The Orb of Truth from her possession, seeking its guidance. With a solemn inquiry, she beseeched, "Pray, which course should we ought to pursue?" A radiant glow emitted from The Orb of Truth, illuminating the path to the left. Hastily reconciling it,

Sarah returned to Abby's side, her voice containing a melodic tone, as she uttered, "Oh Abby…" Intrigued, Abby met her gaze.

Sarah indicated that she would determine the appropriate path, specifically the path on the left. When Abby inquired about her method, Sarah responded succinctly, "While all roads exhibit patterns, the correct path stands apart by conforming to any pattern." Consequently, Abby nodded in agreement, and the two girls proceeded to encounter the second obstacle.

OBSTACLE 2, In stark contrast to the previous realm observed, the current environment presents a notable depiction. It features a magnificent golden gate adorned with intricate carvings depicting the countenance of an elderly woman, alongside dilapidated walls that bear the marks of time's passage and a flourish of moss that gracefully cloaks their surfaces. "Welcome, welcome, my dear children!" warmly utters the elderly woman.

The old woman graces each of them with a radiant, genial smile, prefacing her words with, "Before proceeding through this gateway, you must first embark on the challenge of unraveling my riddle. Are you both willing to embrace this endeavor?" In response, both young girls affirm their readiness by nodding their heads in unison.

With a smile adorning the elderly lady's countenance, she enunciates each word with a sense of conviction. "It eludes sight, eludes touch, eludes sound, and eludes scent. It resides beyond celestial bodies and beneath the undulating terrain, saturating vacant crevices. It precedes and succeeds, extinguishing existence and stifling mirth. What is it?"

The young girls engage in deep contemplation, their minds immersed in the task at hand. After a few minutes, Sarah emerges victorious with her solution. "It's darkness, isn't it?" The old lady's visage brightens with a smile as she confirms Sarah's astute deduction, eliciting a sense of fulfillment and pride in Abby, who witnesses her friend's display of intellect.

OBSTACLE 3, As the girls continued their journey towards the final obstacle, Abby suddenly turned to Sarah. Her eyes welled up with tears and an overwhelming surge of anger threatened to surface. "What happened, Abby?" Sarah inquired, concerned. Abby sprinted a short distance ahead but abruptly halted in her tracks, gathering her emotions before speaking further.

"Nothing went according to plan!" she screamed; her voice filled with frustration. Overwhelmed by her emotions, Abby dropped to her knees and began to cry. Consumed by her stubbornness, Abby continued to shed tears until Sarah intervened, offering a glimmer of hope. "Perhaps fate has something else in store for us," Sarah suggested gently. "But who's to say we can't complete the mission? All we need is focus and teamwork."

As the bright light faded, Sarah and Abby stood before the radiant figure of the Sun Goddess. Her ethereal presence filled the temple, and a sense of awe washed over them.

The Sun Goddess spoke with a melodious voice, "Brave adventurers, you have cleansed the cursed temple and released me from my captivity. I am eternally grateful for your courage and determination."

She extended her hand towards Sarah and Abby, revealing a small, golden key adorned with intricate engravings. "As a token of my gratitude, I grant you the Key to Escape Eternity. With this key, you hold the power to transcend the confines of time and space."

Sarah's eyes widened in astonishment as she accepted the key. She felt its weight in her palm, understanding the significance it held. Abby smiled warmly, acknowledging the profound gift they had received.

The Sun Goddess continued, her voice resonating with wisdom. "This key will open doors to new realms, untold adventures, and paths unexplored. It is yours to wield but use it wisely. Remember that with great power comes great responsibility."

Sarah nodded, her heart filled with a mix of excitement and trepidation. She understood the magnitude of the responsibility bestowed upon her, knowing that their lives would forever be changed by this wondrous gift.

Abby stepped forward and bowed graciously to the Sun Goddess. "Thank you, mighty deity, for your blessings and guidance. We shall honor the trust you've placed in us."

The Sun Goddess smiled radiantly, her form gradually dissolving into shimmering beams of sunlight. "May fortune favor your path, dear adventurers. Go forth and embrace the boundless possibilities that await you."

And with those parting words, the Sun Goddess vanished, leaving Sarah and Abby alone in the temple. They exchanged determined glances, ready to embark on their next journey armed with the Key to Escape Eternity.

7

The Illusion of Riddles

CHALLENGE 2 OBSTACLE 1, As the two girls advance towards the second challenge, a substantial and ominous gate to the second realm swings open, unveiling a labyrinth of intricate design. Upon stepping inside, Sarah's eyes swirl with a mesmerizing shade of purple before abruptly vanishing from sight. Abby found this occurrence peculiar, yet she determinedly pressed on, navigating her way through the perplexing maze.

On the contrary, Sarah's encounter differed significantly from Abby's. She found herself immersed in an enchanting phenomenon, one that was even more captivating and hypnotic than what Abby had just experienced.

Sarah became ensnared in an immersive realm where disconcerting sounds permeated the air. Sinister laughter, anguished cries of pain, and tormented wails echoed around her, mingling with the tears shed by the lost souls. Puzzled and disoriented, she questioned her whereabouts but entertained the possibility that this unsettling experience might be a deliberate trap. Despite her uncertainties, Sarah remained resolved to stay on course alongside her steadfast companion, Abby.

On the contrary, Abby found herself engaged in a fierce confrontation with a monstrous creature endowed with gnashing teeth and eyes as crimson as freshly spilled blood. Its pallid white skin and violet-hued paws added to the creature's foreboding presence. Overwhelmed by fear, Abby grappled with her uncertainty, unsure of how to combat this formidable foe. She searched for a glimmer of hope, desperately seeking a strategy to overcome the daunting challenge before her.

As time elapsed, the resonating cries and laughter grew increasingly resonant for Sarah, gradually morphing into an overwhelming symphony of sound. The relentless onslaught of disconcerting echoes further estranged her from the realm of reality, ensnaring her in a maelstrom of harrowing sensations. Meanwhile, Abby found herself falling victim to the insidious influence of the monster. It cunningly seized control of her mind, distorting her perception to the point where she genuinely believed that the monstrous entity was not an illusion but a tangible presence within their shared reality.

As time seemed to regain its grip on reality, Sarah and Abby persevered through the labyrinthine maze, ardently battling the illusions that plagued their minds. Finally, as they neared the end of their arduous journey, their gazes locked, and a profound sense of astonishment washed over them both. Overwhelmed by a mix of relief and joy, their trembling bodies gave way to tears of sheer elation. In that poignant moment, their shared triumph resonated deeply, solidifying their unbreakable bond and marking the culmination of their extraordinary adventure.

United in celebration, both girls reveled in their hard-earned victory before embarking on their next challenge with renewed determination. With hearts brimming with joy and spirits lifted by their previous success, they pressed forward toward the second obstacle, ready to face whatever trials awaited them with unwavering resolve.

OBSTACLE 2, As the group progresses to the subsequent challenge, Sarah softly murmurs, "I possess neither the ability to remain stagnant nor the capacity to retreat, impervious to the effects of aging experienced by individuals. Through the passage of decades, I am subject to constant remodeling by people." Intrigued, her companion pauses and inquires about her utterance. Sarah responds, "In a newspaper, I once encountered a joke devoid of an accompanying answer. Since then, I have persistently endeavored to unravel its intended meaning."

A sweet, cotton candy-like voice gently emanated, uttering, "Your forthcoming challenge awaits. Time tightly maintains its hold, anticipating your initiative. If you wish to proceed, make your way to Mt. Atropolips." Subsequently, the voice gradually diminished into silence.

With no knowledge of its origin or identity, the girls persisted with unwavering determination and continued their journey.

As they arrived at the summit of Mt. Atropolips, a majestic sight greeted them—a golden trident poised atop the highest peak. Brimming with courage, they embarked on the challenging ascent, scaling the mountain with unwavering determination.

"Not so fast!" a resounding voice exclaimed. Swift as the speed of light, a protective shield enveloped the trident, causing it to radiate a mesmerizing hue of blue light.

As Abby concluded her whispered words to Sarah, a deafening avalanche suddenly erupted from the mountain, violently propelling both of them off its treacherous peak, and leaving them tumbling in chaos.

At that very moment, their gaze fell upon an elderly woman who had collapsed beneath the mountain's imposing presence.

"Oh my!" Abby exclaimed, her voice tinged with shock and concern.

Filled with instinctive compassion, the two girls swiftly rushed to the aid of the fallen woman, eager to offer their assistance.

Extending a helping hand, they assisted the elderly woman to her feet and inquired about her well-being. With great difficulty, she managed to utter, "Food... Water... Shoes... If you have any, please offer them to me!" Her plea carried a sense of desperation and vulnerability.

Without hesitation, they sprang into action, determined to fulfill the woman's urgent needs.

After presenting their offerings, a radiant light emanated from the elderly woman, revealing her true identity as the sun goddess. The girls stood transfixed, awestruck by this revelation. With a gentle smile, the goddess praised their success, affirming that they had overcome the challenge. She proceeded to impart vital knowledge about the significance of the trident and bestowed celestial weapons upon them to aid in their quest and assist her in retrieving the coveted artifact.

RETRIEVING THE GOLDEN TRIDENT, As the girls made their way towards the mountain's peak, their hearts were filled with a combination of excitement and nervousness. Each step brought them closer to their destination, but it also heightened their awareness of the potential dangers that awaited them.

Equipped with their celestial weapons, the girls knew they had the power to overcome any adversary that crossed their path. However, they also recognized the importance of caution and maintaining their balance amidst the treacherous terrain. The falling avalanche served as a constant reminder of the perils they faced.

With each footfall, the ground quivered beneath them, and loose rocks threatened to send them tumbling down the mountainside. They tightly gripped their weapons, using them not only as tools for battle but also as additional support to steady themselves.

Their journey was arduous, but the girls pushed themselves forward, their determination unwavering. They communicated with one another, offering words of encouragement and guidance to ensure they all stayed focused and alert.

As they ascended higher, the air grew thinner, making it even more challenging to catch their breath. But the girls refused to let fatigue overwhelm them. They reminded themselves of their goal—to reach the mountain's peak and fulfill their purpose.

Finally, after what felt like an eternity, they reached the summit. Standing atop the majestic peak, they gazed at the breathtaking view that stretched out before them. It was a moment of triumph and accomplishment, knowing they had conquered both external obstacles and their inner fears.

The girls took a moment to catch their breath, reveling in their success and the strength they had discovered within themselves. They knew that this experience had not only tested their physical abilities but had also forged unbreakable bonds of friendship and courage.

With their celestial weapons still in hand, the girls felt invincible, ready to face whatever challenges lay ahead. Armed with newfound confidence and resilience, they continued their journey, knowing that they were capable of overcoming any obstacle that stood in their way.

As Sarah confidently declared the riddle's answer to the mysterious voice, a sense of anticipation filled the air. The girls knew that their celestial weapons held immense power, and they understood that by combining them, they could unravel the shield that lay before them.

With a synchronized motion, they raised their weapons high, aligning them in perfect harmony. Energy crackled between the weapons as they generated powerful vibrations that radiated outward in all directions. The shield that had concealed their path began to tremble, its once impenetrable surface now showing signs of weakening.

Suddenly, the stillness was shattered as the trident, infused with the energy of their combined weapons, shot towards them with incredible speed. It soared through the air, guided by their focused intention, aimed directly at the shield.

Just as the trident neared its target, a gentle wind enveloped Sarah and her companion, lifting them effortlessly off the ground. Suspended in mid-air, they watched with bated breath as the trident collided with the shield.

A brilliant burst of light erupted upon impact, accompanied by a resounding crack that echoed through the surrounding landscape. The shield shattered into countless fragments, dissipating like mist in the wind.

As the girls were gently lowered back to the ground, they exchanged triumphant glances, their determination and teamwork paying off. They had overcome yet another obstacle on their quest, unlocking a path forward to face whatever awaited them next.

With their celestial weapons still in hand and their spirits invigorated by the victory, they stepped through the remnants of the shattered shield, ready to embrace the challenges and adventures that lay ahead.

The girls exchanged puzzled looks as the voice declared their completion of all three obstacles, even though they were under the impression that they had only faced two. However, their trust in themselves and their instincts urged them to continue, following the guidance of the mysterious voice.

With a mix of curiosity and excitement, they proceeded further, their celestial weapons still at the ready. They traversed through a winding path that led them deeper into the unknown, their senses heightened and hearts filled with anticipation.

As they journeyed onward, the surroundings began to change. The air grew colder, and a dense mist engulfed their surroundings, making it difficult to see what lay ahead. Unease settled over them, but their determination pushed them forward.

Suddenly, the mist cleared, revealing a vast, otherworldly landscape before them. They stood on the precipice of a chasm, its depths shrouded in darkness. A narrow bridge stretched across, seemingly suspended in mid-air, connecting their current position to an unknown destination.

The mysterious voice echoed once again, its tone filled with both challenge and encouragement. "To progress, you must cross this bridge of uncertainty. Trust in yourselves, for your inner strength will guide you."

Sarah and her companion shared a determined glance, silently reaffirming their resolve. With steady steps and unwavering focus, they ventured onto the bridge, each footfall echoing throughout the seemingly endless expanse.

As they advanced, the bridge trembled beneath their weight, adding another layer of trepidation to their journey. Doubts and fears threatened to consume them, but they drew upon the courage they had cultivated throughout their previous challenges.

Their celestial weapons glowed brightly, illuminating their path and casting aside the shadows of uncertainty. Step by step, they pressed forward, relying on their intuition and the bond between them.

Time seemed to stretch, and the echoes of their footsteps resonated in harmony with their racing hearts. Every moment tested their resilience and belief in themselves, but they refused to yield.

Finally, as they reached the other side of the bridge, a surge of triumph surged through their beings. They had conquered the challenge of uncertainty, emerging stronger and more resolute than before.

The mysterious voice echoed once more; its tone filled with admiration. "Well done, brave warriors. You have surpassed the test of uncertainty. Proceed to the final challenge that awaits you."

With renewed determination, Sarah and her companion continued their quest, eager to face the ultimate challenge that awaited them. They were fueled not only by their celestial weapons but also by the unyielding spirit within themselves. Together, they would confront whatever lay ahead, ready to prove their mettle and fulfill their destiny.

The girls stood before the radiant figure of the sun goddess, her presence commanding and awe-inspiring. They had reached the end of their journey, prepared to face the final challenge, and sought the blessing of the sun goddess to carry their celestial weapons.

With humility and respect, they knelt before the divine being, their hearts filled with gratitude for the opportunity bestowed upon them. The sun goddess regarded them with a gentle smile, her eyes shining with wisdom.

"You have proven yourselves worthy," she spoke in a voice that resonated like warm sunlight. "I permit you to wield the celestial weapons on your journey. May their power guide you, protect you, and serve as a beacon of hope in times of darkness."

As she extended her hands towards the girls, rays of golden light emanated from her palms, enveloping their celestial weapons. The weapons glowed with an ethereal brilliance, imbued with the divine energy of the sun goddess.

The girls rose to their feet, their hearts brimming with gratitude and renewed determination. They felt a surge of power coursing through their beings, connecting them to the celestial realm and infusing them with unwavering strength.

"Thank you, great sun goddess," Sarah spoke, her voice filled with reverence. "We shall honor your gift and wield these celestial weapons with courage and responsibility."

The sun goddess nodded approvingly. "Go forth now, brave warriors, and fulfill your destiny. Remember, it is not just the weapons that make you formidable, but the light within your spirits. May you bring balance and harmony wherever your journey takes you."

With a final nod of farewell, the sun goddess disappeared, leaving the girls standing there, ready to embark on their final challenge. Empowered by the blessing and guidance of the sun goddess, they set forth, confident in their abilities and united in their purpose.

Their celestial weapons gleamed with newfound radiance, a tangible reminder of the sun goddess's favor. With each step they took, they carried not only the physical tools but also the essence of divine light within them. They were prepared to face any obstacle that awaited, knowing that the sun goddess's blessing would guide and protect them until they reached the end of their quest.

8

More Illusions

As the girls approached the magnificent palace, they couldn't help but be in awe of its grandeur. The palace stood tall and imposing, with intricate carvings and shimmering golden accents adorning its exterior. It seemed to emanate an otherworldly aura, hinting at the magical challenges that waited inside.

Undeterred by their silent celestial weapons, the girls entered the palace, determined to overcome whatever obstacles lay ahead. As they stepped through the ornate entrance, they found themselves in a vast opulent hall. Little did they know that it was just another illusion trying to trick them. But the inner thought of the illusion was different. In Abby's and Sarah's eyes, they saw the beauty of the castle. The walls were adorned with majestic tapestries depicting mythical creatures and epic battles, while the floor was covered in a mosaic of sparkling gemstones.

At the end of the hall, stood a regal figure in robes of iridescent blue, wearing a crown adorned with sparkly stars. He introduced himself to the girls as the Guardian of the Celestial Palace, a wise and powerful being who tested the worthy adventures seeking passage or a gateway to the next world.

The Guardian explained that to proceed further, the girls would have to prove their word by mastering the Art of Elemental Magic. He presented them with a series of challenges, each focused on harnessing and controlling a different element- fire, water, earth, and air.

With determination in their hearts, the girls embraced the opportunity to learn and grow. They immerse themselves in the challenges, practicing spells, invoking the elements, and honing their newfound abilities. Despite initial struggles, they preserved, finding strength in their unity and unwavering belief in their capabilities.

Gradually their celestial weapons responded to the comments, resonating with the elemental forces they had tamed. Encouraged by their progress, the girls pushed forward, facing one challenge after another, gradually unlocking the mysteries of the palace, improving themselves ready for the guardians' guidance. After all that was over, the girls realized that the image of the castle and the guardian was just an illusion as they watched it dissolve into the thick air.

Being shocked at this mystical view, Sarah eyed the surroundings as the palace dissolved into a forest of thin trees immersing herself in an impressive view. Not only was the forest beautiful, but what they saw was more inspiring. The girls saw centaurs, Deer, and other mythical creatures, and couldn't help but be in awe. It was a view that Abby and Sarah could remember their entire life. Proceeding over to the next challenge, they understood that this particular challenge was to learn the difference between reality and illusions and help them over time.

9

Francesco

After returning from the palace of illusions, Abby and Sarah returned on a stone path. Then out of nowhere approached a tiger. It did look fierce and ready to attack, but Abby wondered if he was just trying to tell them something. But the tiger just obediently sat down and purred. "What the—" Abby thought, but in a minute, they were kidnapped.

"Where are we?" Abby thought to herself. She didn't remember anything from back except the time when they'd stumbled across that innocent tiger. She looked around the dark and dense room but saw nothing but a small lantern, so dim that Abby could barely see anything. Next, it was a door that looked locked and a dark window. Besides her was Sarah sitting unconsciously. When she tried to get up, she couldn't since she didn't feel her hands locked against the chair.

Finally, she gave up and decided to wake Sarah up. She bumped into her chair multiple times, but she didn't wake up. "UGH!" Abby said loudly. That shook Sarah awake because a minute later she made a small yawn. "Ab?" Sarah said softly. "Where are we?" But before she had time to answer anything the door opened.

The man was holding a tray and was now holding the lantern on his head. That was just incredible! Abby couldn't imagine if she'd switched places with that guy, how would she ever manage to do that?

His face was slim, his hair was short and perfectly trimmed, he had a mustache long but short, and facial hair sticking out of his chin. He was wearing a white striped shirt with a green sleeveless coat, black pants, and a red apron. It seemed to Abby that he had either come from Italy or that this place was designed in Italy format. "Good evening my lovely dears!" The man said in a pure Italian accent. "Dinner is served," he said.

Sarah showed fists of anger. "NO!" She screamed, "**WE WON'T EAT ANYTHING UNTIL _YOU_ GIVE US INFORMATION!**" Abby could feel her heart race. She hesitated but carried all courage and said, "Gosh Sarah! ARE YOU OKAY? You need to calm down.! Yes, we are somewhere, yes we are surrounded, yes for everything but you seriously need to chill your anger if you want to avoid causing trouble!"

The guy sighed and took a deep breath before saying, "Okay, I'll tell you all you need to know." Since Sarah was still quite mad, Abby decided to speak for her instead. "Sire, we would like to know your name, who you work for, and why we were brought here?" He shook his head in disdain and said, "I cannot tell you all the information for I shall face severe consequences. However, I can tell you who I am and why I work here."

Abby and Sarah listened to the story for five minutes straight. Abby was most certainly shocked. Surely the mafia boss had a backhand on this slavery and kidnapping stuff. "Now eat up quickly! I have things to do, you know." Francesco said hurriedly. "I will untie your hands and will meet you back in ten minutes." Then he set the trays on two tables and walked behind Sarah and Abby to untie their hands. Abby even wondered if ten minutes was enough to eat.

"Hey Francesco?" she said.

"Yes?" he replied.

"Don't you ever feel like escaping?"

Francesco nodded and left with his hands behind his back and head down. He locked the door and faded into the dark.

Has anyone told you that it feels good to be free? Has anyone told you how trapped and dense it feels when you have less time to eat and one area where you have to sit and look at a single lamp lit? Maybe or maybe not but believe it that is what Abby and Sarah are going through. Imagine when you are given a five-minute task and when you are almost halfway there, a bell rings and that time is up. That is why people say time flies by really fast. And just like that, when Abby and Sarah were almost there to finish what they were given, Francesco came in to check on them. "Are you both done eating?"

"MMM..." Sarah mumbled with her mouth stuffed with pizza bites.

"The food was delicious, but we were not finished eating as we wanted to eat every bite with love and enjoy its taste," Abby spoke nonchalantly.

This made Francesco blush because the second Abby finished talking, he shot his head up and beamed a huge smile on his face and rivers of tears flowing down into a pond of water on the ground. He was struggling to find his words and finally wiping off his tears he spoke, "Th-th-thank you!" he sniffled. "No one has ever appreciated our hard work on making the food. You are the first ones, Abby, and Sarah. I don't know how to thank you more. Because you have made my heart flood with joy, I encourage you to take your time. Ring this bell so that I can come and collect your trays." He stopped by the door and looked back. "I have a plan," he whispered.

After what felt like hours, Abby and Sarah were finally escorted to the bathroom one by one to change into their pajamas. They were each given hand-woven pj's of their choice and had to change as per the rules. Finally, when they were done, they followed Francesco to a bedroom any princess could ever imagine. "WOW!" Abby blurted.

The interior was white with golden outlines, the bedside walls were smokey purple with delicate faint strokes of royal blue, and the bunk beds were stacked on top of each other like a wine dangling from its tree, but unlike the color green it was white with gentle details of golden strokes. The mattress sheet was velvet purple with pink pillows and a quilt of royal blue with an embroidered design colored in purple and pink. Underneath, was a small fluffy velvet carpet, and in front of it was a sofa the exact matching color of the bed. Next to it was a side table with the same materials used, voice-activated wall lights, and an armor and reading light sitting next to it. The bathroom was even more luxurious, unlike an ordinary bathroom. The floor mats were fluffy velvet, the bathtub and sink were graphite gray with a golden faucet, and the towels were silk white. Within the room, there was a closet full of beautiful clothes. It was fascinating! Abby and Sarah were shocked and in awe. He then turned off the lights other than the voice-activated and locked the room.

10

Yay! Let's Escape!

At 1:03 AM in the city of Satin Rose, a hushed urgency filled the air as Francesco, a flame seemingly lit atop his head, quietly urged his companions to awaken. As the soundless clinks of jangling keys reached their ears, Abby was first to rouse from her slumber, rubbing her tired eyes, and noticing a blurry Francesco before her. Struggling to find her words in a drowsy state, Abby managed "Fran... Francesco? Are we to make our escape now?" Francesco nodded in affirmation, demonstrating his intention to carry out the plan in utmost silence. Sarah, still groggy, was roused by Abby's silent scream. " What, Abby? What's going on?" Abby shoots a glance at Sarah. Francesco and Sarah quickly grasped the plan.

Addressing Francesco, Abby respectfully inquired, "Francesco we would appreciate it if you could join us inside to discuss your plan." Francesco obliged, entering the room and shutting the door with utmost caution. Placing a printout on the table and extending a torch, he offered his apologies for the earlier interruption before proceeding to outline their course of action. " First and foremost," he began, pausing to clear his throat, " we shall make our way to the nearby words where you were initially held captive. However, we must exercise caution, as the night goes patrolled in the dark woods. Rumors abound of dangerous creatures and spirits inhabiting the forest, causing most to shy away from venturing there."

As they drew nearer to the hallway exit, an unexpected twist occurred - Abby, Sarah, and Francesco found themselves adored in a charming, yellow sundress and matching sandals. Their tents were abruptly halted as two guards confronted them. " and Mr. Francesco, movie inquire as to your destination with the prisoners?" Asked one guard leaving Francesco baffled. " "The master directed me to go with the girls to his laboratory, so I was walking them there," replayed Francesco, his response prompting a bewildered thought from Sarah – " he has a laboratory?"

Stepping forth undeterred from the guards, Abby, Sarah, and Francesco pressed onward toward the ominous words that loomed before them. The foreboding surroundings within the depths of the city of satin rose, imported a sense of trepidation for us to walk through this desolated expanse. Tall, gaunt trees seemed to converge, obscuring the dark in the sky, and nearly a full moon behind a veil of clouds, misleading its appearance to the mere crescent. The grass, Overgrown and prickly, Brushed against their legs with every step, while the muddy terrain clung to their shoes with unruly stickiness. After what felt like an arduous journey, their weary feet brought them to a sealed entry. Francesco, contemplating the situation, stretched his thin thoughtfully.

Upon wearing the necklace bestowed upon them, a luminous yellow light was emitted, subsequently breaking the seal and unleashing the dark forest.

11

The Dark Forest - Abby's Experience

During our journey through the dark forest, both Sarah and I were filled with trepidation as spirits continuously passed by us. It was in this unsettling atmosphere that we encountered Avery, a spectral entity known to Francesco. She revealed herself as a lost soul seeking guidance and retribution to summon the powerful figures of the Hell King and Haven Queen. As Francesco recounted Avery's tale, I found myself overcome with intense emotions, shedding tears uncontrollably. Even Avery seemed to empathize with the depth of my sorrow.

"Okay okay! Stop, please stop!" I told Francesco before turning to Avery. "Avery, I am so *so* sorry!" I did mean it.

"Francesco faced severe harassment due to my sacrifice for love, leaving me deeply impressed, similar to your demeanor, Abby. However, I can't recall the events surrounding my death and there appears to be confusion regarding the circumstances I encountered. Regrettably, such a situation occurred."

"So then Avery, to summon the gods of the underworld, what type of vengeance do you have to seek?"

"I have to get revenge against the second-generation disciple of my murderer."

"Ok, so what exactly are we planning to do?" Said Sarah.

We all look up at her. She did have a point. But fairly, it was not the time to argue, it was time to think and act. Avery looked so pale that she was going to... uh I don't know. Okay okay, back to the topic.

"Avery," I spoke in a gentle tone. She looked up. "I know it is hard for you, but if we are going to avenge the disciple of _your_ killer, then how are we going to know who it is, and who is the right person we have to sacrifice?" At this point forward, Avery was fiddling with her hair before looking back up. But before she could answer, Sarah piped her head in.

"Francesco, is it only girls that stay captive, or so do boys?" Sarah said, looking up at me and then Avery.

"Ah! Now you see, that is a very good question." But before Francesco said anything, we saw a hurdle of wardens coming our way. "Hide!" Francesco whispered in an alert.

12

The Dark Forest- Francesco's Experience

I took the girls to a safe hideout. Because Avery was a ghost, she accepted to scare away those wardens. "Muahahaha! Hello little fellas. What have you gotten meeeeeeee!?" The second Avery finished speaking, we heard a moaning scream. I looked at a peek and saw the guards running away from Avery frightened. I escorted the girls into a secret passage that only *I, Avery and our master's son* knew about. On the way, I explained why I was forced to join Master the background story of her. Of course, Abby and Sarah seemed a little emotional than Avery but she accepted her fate and my fate. I do feel bad, aster, but what else choice do I have but to help her? We then ended up in a small tunnel where they found a room. "We will sleep here, and Avery, you please go ahead and get us some food. I leave you two out and you can change your nighties."

Later that night I asked Avery to keep a watch. So far, nothing has happened. The next morning Avery bought some food. We ate up and we changed. Of course, we didn't have a shower, so we were all stinking. Abby remained silent all along the path, and I thought that she might have something she didn't want to discuss.

And then all of a sudden Sarah beamed in. She happily told us that she had a way to get us free from this mess. I'd hoped the master wouldn't find us here. But even this is a place that *we* haven't yet discovered, so how could the master find us? Anyway, we sat and listened to Sarah's plan.

Abby always recounted how smart and intelligent she was, but the more I got to know them, I felt Abby was right at one point. I can't be jealous though, Avery was also the same.

13

Sarah's Way Out

"Okay, so here is what we are going to do. Avery, you are going to call all your spirit friends." She nodded. "Francesco returns to the mansion and tells your master that we escaped. Meanwhile, Avery and her friends will block the path to the dark forest. Abby and I will take the way out of the tunnel and hide in the nearby cemetery." I lost track while looking at Avery. Abby spoke for the first time this morning. "Sarah, how do you know that there is a nearby cemetery?",

"Uh, no time. Continuing, when _your_ master is being distracted Francesco sneaks in the same tunnel. Time is ticking. Get your move on now, and for, you Avery, make sure you have enough friends to block his/her path." They nodded at me and left immediately.

I then looked over Abby who looked bewildered. I motioned her and we too left the tunnel.

We reached the cemetery an hour later. By that time, I had kept a tracker on Francesco. His location showed in the tunnel where we started. Abby and I decided to venture out and explore this new location. Abby was thirsty so she told me she was going to look for spring water, and that we'd meet back here. It was expectable, a fair deal. I ventured deeper into the forest and saw many beautiful creatures. It was splendButterflies were roaming around, deers eating grass, tall and beautiful trees, and flowers with an aroma that made it hysterical. The river was flowing down elegantly and the fire in the fire pit danced gracefully. The trees danced in the wind so gracefully.

I laid down on its lovely grass enduring every moment of the fresh breeze that rubbed against my face. I closed my eyes, but then abruptly shot upwards remembering that Abby and Francesco could be anywhere now. I hurriedly went back to the cemetery, but gladly Abby was there talking with Francesco.

It looked like she had found some food and water and came along with Avery. "Oh, hey Sarah!" I recognized that voice— it was Avery. Step forward and meeting my gaze upon hers, I smiled back and waved her hi. Avery was much happier than before, and I was glad.

We had some food and took turns using the bathroom. And once we finished, I led them to the garden I had found. Unexpectedly, the surroundings changed, taking us into the realm of the first element – Earth.

14

The Battle With Elements

The contest, in reactions of Abby and Sarah to the mesmerizing garden, creates an intriguing dynamic. While Abby is enthralled by its magical beauty, there is a perplexing hint of an underlying mystery. The combination of awe and disturbance, and set the scene for further exploration, awaiting the unrevealing of the garden's secrets.

While Francesco and Avery were laughing and giggling, Abby and Sarah saw its mesmerizing beauty and lost in their thoughts, Atrippedrips over a tree bark flew into the air! But just then *swoosh!* Came in a – *fairy*? She elegantly landed on two legs with her wings dropped down. She let down Abby and walked away. Soon she returned with some herbs. She lifted Abby's skirt squeezed the liquid and spread it around her leg. "This should help you heal." She then turned away and flew inside a small door drilled inside a tree trunk.

Abby got up and hugged her best friend. "I'm okay, strawberry." She said before Sarah could speak anything. "I know Ab, but we are like a – _we are _a family. How do you expect me not to get worried?" when Sarah said that; it made Abby fall into deep sorrow.

Although it may have been awkward, Sarah realized that this was not what it looked like. It was a test. "ABBIEE! STOP RIGHT THERE! COME OUT FROM THAT ROOM!" she looked dazzled as she crept her head towards that direction. "One moment please." As soon as she stepped out, she felt so dizzy, that she'd fainted.

AIR ELEMENT- "What happened guys? Why are we here? I thought that we were in a garden and…" she trailed off. "…And I don't remember anything further." Sarah shook her head. "Ab don't worry, what we went through was just an illusion. For passing the test, we even got a gem for this next one. Just look around you!" Abby indeed looked around. Sure, it was a different scenario, sure it was condensing, and sure it was dark and gloomy. Many things did seem different. "What? How?" Avery looked at Abby and sighed. "You'll never know," she spoke.

The gang stormed off immediately into the damp rainforest. Just then, an ambush of sharp wind came in and they were being pushed backwards; – except Avery of course. Avery turned back to find her friends in a fizzy situation and called an emergency meeting for her ghostly friends. Together, they double-hold each person and swam across the air until they found dry land.

In an immersing bright light, a fairy appeared. She seemed to lose control of her powers because everywhere she went there would be a burst of wind flying around like a crazy tornado. Avery remembered the stone, pulled it out, and foreshadowed trees trapping the wind. Later a jewel appeared within the hands of Abby herself. "Thank you." The three said and left for the next realm. The gateway to the fire fairy.

FIRE REALM- The arid atmosphere enveloped the explorers as they penetrated the realm, where scorched trees and a fiery red sky created an infernal landscape, emanating intense heat with each step. Unbeknownst to them, a fairy observed their every move from the concealment of a cave.

"Here are my pretty children." She said, sneering. "What could they possibly want from me?"

The next view shocked Abby, Sarah, Francesco, and Avery. The woods were on fire and boiling lava erupted from beneath. As they backed away from the scene, a figure in red emerged from the dark.

They turned around in shock. The dress had flame embroidery, tall red heels, and a cape covering her face. She smiled sinisterly at the four as she walked down the aisle. "Hello, love." She said, eyeing Francesco, who was shaking through his spine. He wanted to back off from whoever, though it felt to him like his legs had been tied to the ground, disabling him from moving. The 'Red Lady' got closer and her sinister laughter inhaled the scared kids.

Amid the unsettling scene, Abby introduced herself and her friends—Francesco, Avery, and her cousin Sarah—to the enigmatic figure known as the 'Red Lady,' who had emerged amidst the fiery woods. Despite their fear, Abby managed to convey their identities with a noticeable quiver in her voice.

Fiammetta, also known as Fia, responded with a sinister laugh, revealing her striking features—gorgeous white skin adorned with dark red lipstick and fiery eyeliner. Despite her intimidating appearance, Abby discerned a profound sense of sorrow, agony, and loneliness in Fia's fiery eyes.

"Listen Fia- I mean Fiammetta," Abby said, pausing, which led Fiammettas eyes to land her gaze upon her. "I'm listening," she said, "and please I'd love it when people say my name as Fia more than Fiammetta." Abby nodded, giving Sarah a quick gaze of assurance. "Let's make a deal." Fiammetta's eyes sparkled with hope. She pounced up on her legs and moved closer to Abby. Of course, she was scared but did she have a choice? "Anyways," she continued, "if you tell us your problem, we may be able to help you. And if we do successfully help you, you have to promise to let us go. Do we have a deal?"

Fiammetta thought for a second. Did someone really offer her help? Was she finally going to get back the life she once had? She then nodded her head in agreement.

Narrator: *The four — no wait five, sat down to negotiate more about their deal.*

Upon Francesco's suggestion, they engaged in a conversation with Fiammetta. Utilizing the two gems in their possession, they conjured an enchanting forest with vibrant creatures and crafted a fiery dwelling for her. Fiammetta, momentarily captivated by the unfolding scene, expressed her gratitude before permitting them to proceed to the next realm with the heart of Fire.

WATER REALM- The transition from the fiery realm to the emerging frozen water realm caught Francesco, Abby, and Sarah off guard, leaving them shivering in the cold. Initially anticipating a straightforward mission of rewarming the ocean, they soon realized their task extended to liberating the imprisoned water queen. The unforeseen challenges made them question the perceived ease of their mission.

Abby harnessed the power of the Heart of Fire to liberate the ocean from its icy restraints, bringing warmth and relief to the once-frozen waters. Despite their successful intervention to free the ocean, uncertainty lingered as Francesco, Abby, and Sarah remained unsure about the whereabouts of the water goddess.

Opting to enhance their search efficiency, Francesco, Abby, and Sarah decided to split up in their quest to locate the water goddess, understanding that finding her would significantly facilitate their mission. The absence of a communication source posed a challenge, and navigating the vast ocean without a map added to their uncertainty. Despite these obstacles, they pressed on with determination in their ongoing journey.

Abby- While traversing the expansive ocean, I witnessed the extensive destruction of corals and sea life. Upon reaching the eastern region, devoid of immediate threats to the water goddess or the ocean, I pondered whether the mystery behind this devastation extended beyond the current realm. The vastness of the ocean made it challenging to discern.

After about three hours, I retraced my steps, using seashells as markers to navigate back to our starting point. Upon returning, I sought refuge on a nearby island, where I changed into warmer attire and prepared essential survival items for the anticipated challenges ahead.

Sarah- Venturing West revealed a tranquil and uneventful journey, devoid of apparent threats. The fish moved swiftly, seemingly in a hurry, but no signs of harm were evident. Finding no pertinent clues, I retraced my steps and unexpectedly encountered Abby on a small island. In a shared moment of laughter and conversation, we waited for the rest of the group to reunite.

Avery- As a ghost, my ethereal passage through the water allowed me to easily navigate to where the water goddess was imprisoned. Recognizing the vital role of the water jewel in progressing through the realm and fulfilling our mission, I observed the scene and received a set of instructions before being sent back. Reuniting with Abby and Sarah, we spent the waiting time joyfully, anticipating Francesco's arrival.

Francesco- Struggling to navigate the water, I grappled with the challenges, realizing the journey ahead wouldn't be easy. Faced with waning hope, I retraced my steps to reunite with Abby and the rest of the group.

Avery explained everything that was told to her and without waiting a second the crew headed further out.

What took four hours, they were finally able to move on. "According to the map," Abby said in dismay, "we are 'supposed' to meet the king of hell, which should be a reddish-golden gate to enter his realm." Avery then interrupted Abby's deep thoughts on the map which had shaken her. "At that point on, I might be able to summon him and the Queen of Heaven to get my immortal peace." They glanced at her. "But weren't you supposed to find whatever person to seek vengeance, Avery?" Sarah glanced over at her. "Yes, but..." Avery then explained what happened in the castle when they were in the dark forest. "His soul drives with me further into, and innocence will be granted as well as mortal peace to me." "Oh," they all spoke at once. "Take the lead, Avery!"

15

The King of Hell- Avery's Experience

The squad and I were just about to enter when suddenly... *BOOM!* A group of demons surrounded us. They flew around demanding stuff from us to prove our identities. "STOP IT RIGHT THERE!" Abby said frantically. The demons had stopped and crept closer to Abby. I was feeling nervous about what could happen.

"Three mortals, eh?" Demon 1 said.

"I suspect that — someone! Wanna explain something to us?" Demon 2 said, chuckling.

The others grouped in but were soon interrupted by Demon 1 who looked like the main leaders.

"I am—" Sarah said, shuttering her words.

Demon 9 piped up. "Were we talking to you, young mortal?"

Sarah shook her head.

"Ok then, KEEP QUIET!"

After Abby introduced themselves, the conversations kept going on.

"Listen," Sarah said now annoyed, "we are on an extremely important quest, and we have less than five days to return to the mortal world. We really need to speak to the King of Hell and summon the Goddess of Heaven, I believe so?" She then turned to me and I nodded in a comforting way. "Of course, of course. All mortals say the same thing and it is quite boring." Demon 5 said. Demon 1 motions the rest to head back to duty and summons Demon 9 to tell their master about the situation.

Moments later, he swooshed in and brought us inside. "Demon Bones explained to me your whereabouts and it is really undevilish-like." The Hell King spoke. "But I have also been informed about this by the guardian—" he paused to look at Avery and Francesco. "About these two, what is their purpose for coming here?" I gulped through my transparent pale skin and my corpse began to tremble. " I am Avery Kevinsz, and I came here once, remember me?"

The king looked at Avery and laughed. "Oh, it's you. Have you brought the soul yet to prove his or her innocence?" I nodded again, this time having spine-chilling goosebumps driving through the floated dress. "Of course, your Sire."

He took a closer look at the man floating behind Avery. "Is he brought unconscious here?" Abby said, confused.

I nodded immediately not wanting to hint or point out anything to the demon king.

"Name please!" He demanded.

"Your Sire, please accept my apologies but I do not know his name." The look on the king's face could tell me that this case may be complicated and time-consuming.

"Demon Bones, why don't you take a closer look at him? Perhaps you could be useful in a way." The king sneered.

The demon nodded and took a look at the man before whispering something in his ears.

During the process, I floated away, leaving space between the man and the demon.

The king nodded and read his book of death. He said, "According to this book, his name is Joseph, and his innocence is proven that he is not like his father, your disciple, or murderer." I Silently took a deep breath before saying, " Does that mean I'll finally get justice in peace?" The demon nodded approvingly.

"However, the circumstances match that you are given two options to choose from." I waited till the day it finally came. "Option one is," he continued, "to take a rebirth and forget all of your memories while living happily in a wealthy or poor family or! Returning to your real form and enjoying your time on earth."

It was a tough choice.

"If you choose to be reborn, you stay here with me. And if you change to your original form then we must summon the Heaven Queen. So my dear, choose wisely

or else consequences must be paid."

I was battling emotions and had no idea what to choose. I had a wonderful life with Francesco but now was it time to leave already? Will my parents accept me back? I decided it was time for me to leave. I know that someday I will meet him again. "I choose to leave this painful life and rebirth in a poor yet happy family!"

Everyone turned to me and I could see tears flowing in Francesco's eyes.

"But, I will not leave until I help my friends."

The demon king could see the stubbornness in my eyes so he let me go. Then turned to Abby, Sarah, and my dearest Francesco.

"And what about you three?" He asked.

"Me and Sarah," began Abby, "are here to surpass your challenges to take the time clock from the guardian to escape eternity and save the past." Seeing their determination the demon surpassed this realm.

"I am Francesco, and I'm here to support my friends on their journey. If you may allow me to it will be my greatest gratitude. I'm willing to trade in 10 years of my life." The King looked stunned. He accepted the trade and let them all leave.

I stayed and wished them well, a safe journey, and good luck to escape eternity and save the past.

16

Back to The Guardian

"Enter through this portal and it will lead you back to The Guardian." The King said. A portal opened flashing before their eyes as Francesco and Avery waved their arms through mid-air As Sarah and Abby stepped in, they could hear faint conversations between Francesco and the king.

The girls traversed a temporal realm, witnessing the continuum of past, present, and future. The profound shock lingered as they pondered the alterations to the narrative. Questions of elapsed days and missed nights raced through their minds until they reached a standstill. Before them stood the familiar golden gates, marking their return to the starting point.

Amidst contemplation, Abby questioned the feasibility of escaping eternity unaided, acknowledging the impossibility yet harboring a determination to make it a reality. They entered the gates and patiently awaited the reawakening of The Guardian.

The golden drops poured in and out until they melted the marbled statue of The Guardian.

"Well, well. Who do we have here? If it isn't those who solved the mystery and earned the time clock?" The Guardian stiffened himself in a straight position.

The girls nodded. "I'm still wondering how you two solve each realm of challenge without calling for help?" The Guardian continued, "I have been watching the journey of you girls and I don't know if you realized something?" Perhaps not. Thought Abby. Sarah stood there blanked and both girls had a dazzled expression.

"No, we don't know what you are talking about." Abby finally spoke to The Guardian while looking at Sarah.

He chuckled. "Francesco and Avery were also a challenge to see your kindness, persuasion, and determination. You were not delicate and stood out to help. As a result, they helped you cross the challenges and surpass the Demon King. He also looked quite impressed. I got a message from the Satyr Tribe. You've done an outstanding job, therefore, you can be able to use the time clock and save the past. Remember you only get three days to work. The time there is different than the time here, so the clock will also help you know how many days are left. The Portal of Eternity had last opened two decades ago, and if that's where you are planning to start. That's all I can tell you kiddos."

He got up and went over to a celestial ball that contained the time clock. Abby's creation and determination wwereall that had helped throughout their journey. She was more than shocked. Now, she had an opportunity to escape eternity and save the past.

"You can use this whenever you are ready and if you wish, then take this portal and it will teleport you back to the mortal world." The Guardian mumbled.

17

What's Next on Our Cake?

Narrator- *Abby and Sarah take the portal back home and each lies on their beds proud and happy. Abby got the time clock, and escaped eternity, while Sarah enjoyed the fact that she could help her cousin.*

While lying in her bed, Abby twiddled with her hair and thought about their impossible mission. Not only that, she felt more than ready to go into the past and save her family. She finally feels that comes with the memories of Francesco, Avery, Sarah, her mom, and her dad deep within her heart. She couldn't wait to start another chapter with fresh starts.

The one thing that bothered her the most was, would her parents would forget her. Will she restart her life as a twelve-year-old girl? Will her best friend still remember her? She didn't know, but the fact she knew it was worth a try.

18

Abby

2 DAYS LATER- *Bzzzz! Bzzzz! Bzzzz!* *Yawns* Good morning, everyone! Today promises to be amazing because Sarah and I are set to break free from eternity and reshape the past. But first things first—I—oh! It's Sarah's text. "Hurry and get ready, I'm meeting up at your house at 10 a.m. sharp." What! How did I oversleep?

To kick things off, I'm about to use a time clock to finally meet my family. In case you're unfamiliar, let me explain. But first, let's see what's on Sarah's mind.

"Hey Ab, how's it going?"

"Well not a bad morning, just overslept. Now I need to say something so please wait for me by the couch."

"Okay."

Where were we again? Oh right, what was the time clock? Hmm... the time clock is basically a clock where you can set a day and time and even which month or year you want to go on. After setting the time clock, we enter a portal and wala we have entered that time of the year. We have to go back to 2010, the year the portal opened and sucked up many people such as my mom. Now it is time to jump inside the portal, right?

Walks over to the couch.

"Who were you talking to Ab?"

"Oh uh, no one!"

"Well, what were you baffling out there?"

"Oh, I was talking to my lovely reader to get the idea of the time clock."

"Hmm okay, what's the plan now?"

Narrator- Faint sounds of conversation blocked the room as Abby and Sarah stepped inside the portal of time."

19

Echoes of Time

Within the ethereal confines of the Time Reservation realm, Abby and Sarah found themselves engulfed in a swirling vortex of temporal energy. Colors danced and twisted around them as if the very fabric of reality were unraveling before their eyes. The air crackled with electricity, sending shivers down their spines as they ventured deeper into this surreal landscape.

Every step they took seemed to echo through the corridors of time itself, reverberating with the echoes of past and future. Strange whispers filled the air, speaking of forgotten ages and lost civilizations, their words both enchanting and chilling to the bone.

As they traversed through the ever-shifting maze of the Time Reservation, they encountered creatures beyond imagination: beings of pure energy that danced on the edges of perception, their forms shifting and morphing with each passing moment. The very ground beneath their feet seemed to pulsate with life, a living tapestry woven from the threads of time itself.

And then, they stumbled upon the Gate of Ages, a towering monolith that stood as a gateway between worlds. Its surface shimmered with an otherworldly glow, beckoning them closer with promises of untold wonders and unimaginable dangers.

With trembling hands, they reached out and grasped the ancient runes that adorned the gate, feeling the power of centuries coursing through their veins. As they stepped through the threshold, they felt themselves being pulled into the swirling maelstrom of time, their senses overwhelmed by the cacophony of sights and sounds that assailed them from all sides.

But amidst the chaos, they clung to each other, their bond a beacon of hope in the darkness. For they knew that whatever trials awaited them beyond the gate, they would face them together, united in their quest for truth and adventure in this realm of endless possibilities.

20

Oh No! Where is The Guardian?

As Abby and Sarah entered, the portal rotated, displaying a spectrum of vivid colors. Having traversed the Time Reservation realm, Abby and Sarah arrived in the golden realm. Recognizing the familiar surroundings, they entered two golden gates, only to discover an unexpected absence – The Guardian was nowhere to be found on his throne.

Perplexed, Abby and Sarah began searching the area, hoping to locate The Guardian.

Despite thorough searching, The Guardian remained elusive. "Sarah, perhaps it's the right time to contact Satyr," Abby suggested. Sarah agreed, and Abby retrieved the conch bestowed upon them during their last encounter with The Guardian.

Shortly after, a distinct Satyr, unlike any they had encountered before, entered the golden realm. "How may I assist you?" he inquired. Abby spoke up, expressing their uncertainty about The Guardian's whereabouts. Sarah joined in, emphasizing the urgency of their situation and the dire need for The Guardian's assistance.

"Very well. I shall investigate how I can assist you, fine maidens," declared the Satyr before swiftly departing, leaving the girls perplexed. As they prepared to follow him, the Satyr returned in a rush.

"I forgot to mention, fine maidens," he said, looking at Abby and Sarah, "there's a waiting room at the far end of the throne room. You may wait for me there, or remain here. However, I must insist you refrain from attempting to follow me. Understand?"

The girls nodded, and once more, the Satyr hurried away, leaving them bewildered.

After a five-minute wait, Satyr returned, accompanied by The Guardian. "I apologize for the delay; I had a prior meeting with the time clock. Do you still possess it?" Abby searched her bag and presented the Time Clock. Both The Guardian and Sarah smiled.

"Perfect. Now, I shall instruct you on the next steps," The Guardian stated. "However, I must clarify that the first time you summoned the Great Old Satyr doesn't count, as it wasn't related to the quest. Also, be cautious, he tends to be a bit grumpy." The Guardian paused. "

Anyway," he continued, sniffling his nose, "let's proceed."

22

Now What?

A bby scribbles in her diary- "So, I and Sarah ended up following 'The Guardian' in another realm. It was also a much more familiar realm than the one we passed. And what we encountered next was quite shocking for the two of us."*

The Guardian extended a polite greeting, addressing King Demogorgon with a smile. "Well, well, if it isn't my good old friend, Guardian Gabriel," chuckled King Demogorgon. Abby's mind was consumed with questions about The Guardian's concealed name, the veracity of Gabriel, and the trustworthiness of King Demogorgon.

"We are here today to help these young adventurous kids to help save the past and escape eternity. Would you mind coming in for a meeting?"

"Why of course Guardian Gabriel, where are we headed today?"

"Well, it's pretty rare to see you agreeing on something. So I suggest, why not go into a more personal realm?"

"Hmm, I suppose. Let's proceed."

The girls and King Demogorgon followed the 'The Guardian', Guardian Gabriel into a realm that neither of them had seen. "Welcome to the Realm of Time." Guardian Gabriel spoke. "Here we perform certain rituals to activate the Time clock. You must be wondering why I have brought you here, right King Demogorgon?" The demon king nodded his head.

"Well, you will have to open the death circle in order to activate memories set from the past. While you do that I will be reading spiritual spells and absorb the Time Clock's energy. Meanwhile, Abby and Sarah will represent Yin and Yang and help with both energies."

Abby scribbles in her diary- *"And so just like that, we began the rituals and séances."*

23

Going Back In Time

It took one timely hour to complete the full rituals and activate the Time Clock. Finally, when it was time to go, Abby started to cry. "What happened Ab?" Sarah inquired. At this point, Guardian Gabriel and King Demogorgon were starting to get tense. Sarah signaled Guardian Gabriel to give them time alone. He stepped back respecting their privacy.

"Ab, listen to me. We have three minutes to discuss this and step into the portal before it shuts back down. So tell me, what is going on Ab?" Sarah spoke in a soft voice.

"I don't know, strawberry. I'm just scared. What if we fail the mission? What if things don't go as planned? What if we don't escape eternity and save the past? What if I never get to see my parents ever again?" She sobbed more.

Sarah could understand her sorrow but at this moment she had no idea how to comfort her cousin. "It's ok Abby. We should have faith in God and faith in our future. People are relying on us for help. Whether our mission fails or is successful, we are helping thousands of people in Mischief County, think about that."

"Yes you are right," Abby said this time more fiercely, "let's go and escape this together!"

Then, Sarah got up to see the portal closing. She pulled Abby's hand and ran, making her fine braided hair fly in the air. They managed to enter the portal just in time before it shut down.

MARCH 25 2010, MISCHIEF COUNTY 5:00 A.M. - The girls landed in front of their house where Abby could hear her 12-year-old voice talking to her mother. "Mom, the bully, she ripped my favorite dress because she found it so ugly. She was suspended for a month but now it's ruined."

"Oh it's ok honey, perhaps I can restyle it for you."

"Will you mommy? Promise?"

"Haha of course honey."

Fast forward seven hours. Abby and Sarah overhear Abby's mom talking with her dad. "I'm afraid we won't be able to keep the secret from her for much longer. We have to shut down the portal to keep her safe." Her mom said tensed. "We will honey, but that will risk our lives. She doesn't have any relatives. Sarah's family won't accept her." Her dad replied. "Fine!" Snapped Abby's mom. "If you won't, then I will sacrifice myself. Rot to hell." Then her mother stormed out crying.

For the first time, Abby felt sad. She could have imagined what she would have felt if she were in a situation at that age. She knew that whatever could be done, had to be done before the time repeats itself.

"Sarah, our parents sacrificed themselves to protect us, and we have to stop them. We have to find out what we should be able to do as an alternative." Sarah eyed Abby confused. "So?"

"Follow me" and so Sarah did. "This was my favorite hideout that nobody except me knew. I think we should be safe here. Back to the point, a legend of the portal of eternity has a prophecy. It states, 'Those who dare to close the gateway must pay the price with a sacrifice, and in doing so, they shall unravel the secrets of reversing the clock.' Thinking about the prophecy—"

"Abby no offense but I think your younger version is coming this way."

"Hide!"

"Who are you two?—Hello?— I know you two are alive. If you won't tell me who you are, then imma tell momma."

"Oh no!" Thought Abby. "Think fast."

"I am the future you. I come from the life of eternity. Mother hasn't told you yet, because what happens in the future, you— I mean we will lose our parents."

"I'm Sarah, the future version of Sarah, and adding on to future Abby, we are here to fix that so that when you grow older, your future will have changed."

"Now promise me past Abby, whatever happens, don't inform mother about this and avoid her from doing anything crazy, ok?"

Abby from the past nodes her head. "Good girl."

She gets up to leave. When Sarah and Abby are alone in the hideout, they try to interpret the prophecy. Soon they understood what to do and just had to wait for the right time.

The next morning Abby and Sarah were awakened by cold bacon. "Eww." Snorted Sarah. "Better than nothing." The girls ate up and sneaked around the house. Finally, at around 2 pm, their house was left empty. They headed downstairs to the basement where the portal was held. Together, they shattered the piece of glass weakening its portal in energy. And a while later there was a blackout.

24

New Chapter

The next thing Abby saw when she woke up from the blackout was a living room. "Oh, you're awake honey." Said a familiar voice. "Mom is that you?" Abby pondered. "Yep, it's me. You saved me, you saved the world, Abby. You helped shut down the portal. Thank you, thank you so much."

All Abby could react to that was a faint smile. "Now eat up, I have a lot of catching up to do."

"Mom?"

"Yes?"

"Is Sarah ok? Where is dad?" How was your experience in the portal? Have we really escaped eternity?"

"The answer to all of that is yes, and your dad is with Sarah for some time. Her parents were injured while at the portal and had to be hospitalized. She is in depression so he decided to help her. And in the meantime, I will tell you all about my journey in the portal of eternity. I'm proud of you for who you have become. I have never forgotten you."

Abby's mom ruffled Abby's curled hair. "Why don't you first eat up, get refreshed, and then we will talk about it. Hmm?"

And that's how Abby escaped eternity and helped save the past.

The end

Acknowledgement:

The author extends heartfelt gratitude to esteemed best-selling authors who have served as a tremendous source of inspiration for the creation of the book. It is sincerely hoped that readers of all ages will find joy in the narrative, rich with mysteries and friendships. The author's passion for reading and writing has fueled the inception of this work, drawing from a wellspring of creative ideas and thoughts. The belief is that delving into the realm of imagination can be both enjoyable and instrumental in fostering the creation of one's literary works.

The following authors are acknowledged and credited for playing a pivotal role in influencing the storytelling:

- Sarah Mlynowski, author of "Whatever After - Series"
- Roshini Chokshi, author of "The Aru Shah Series"
- K.R Alexander, author of "The Collector Series"
- Betty G. Birney, author of "The World According to Humphrey Series"
- J.K Rowling, author of the "Harry Potter" series
- W. Bruce Cameron, author of "A Dog's Purpose" series

It is important to note that this listing is not intended for purposes of copyright or plagiarism but rather as a recognition of favorite series that have fueled the imaginative process. These authors have been instrumental in shaping the story, and their influence has been invaluable as the author embraces the role of a storyteller.

Additionally, profound appreciation is expressed to the author's parents for their unwavering support, which has been instrumental in bringing this narrative to fruition. It is trusted that immersing oneself in this book will prove to be a heartwarming experience. Sincere thanks are extended for reading, and anticipation is expressed for sharing more of Abby's and Sarah's adventures in future publications.

Learn More About The Author:

In the depths of an arduous recovery from a sports injury at just 12 years old, Fiona D. Mahadkar found solace in the creation of "Escape from Eternity." This poignant tale, born from the crucible of adversity, not only captures her unwavering resilience but also encapsulates the essence of Abby and Sarah's profound journey. Fueled by an unyielding desire for healing and the pursuit of joy, Fiona seeks the unwavering support and heartfelt contributions of kindred spirits to weave more emotionally gripping adventures. With each purchase, readers are not merely spectators but active participants in Fiona's remarkable narrative, becoming integral to spreading the transformative power of resilience and hope to every corner of the globe.

Why did the author choose to publish her book on her birthday?:

The author decided to release their book on their birthday to create a meaningful connection between the two events. They aimed to make their first book launch a memorable celebration on their special day.

Thank you!

Fiona D. Mahadkar [Original Creator of this content.]

"Your quest stirs the dormant power within, awakening your inner strength."
-The Guardian

ESCAPED
"YOUR QUEST STIRS THE DORMANT POWER WITHIN, AWAKENING YOUR INNER STRENGTH."
-THE GUARDIAN
FOR AGES 0-20

www.ingramcontent.com/pod-product-compliance
Lightning Source LLC
Chambersburg PA
CBHW051254160726
47994CB00003B/1164